# When You Wander

## A Search-and-Rescue Dog Story

Margarita Engle

Illustrated by Mary Morgan

Henry Holt and Company

New York

Author Acknowledgments

I thank God for dog noses and search-and-rescue volunteers. I am grateful to
Curtis, Maggi, Chance, Dr. Cheryl Waterhouse, the National Search Dog Alliance,
the California Rescue Dog Association, the National Association for Search and Rescue,
Madera County Search and Rescue, Kai Hernandez, Norma Snelling, Nancy Acebo,
the Hug-a-Tree Foundation, Reka Simonsen, Noa Wheeler, Laura Godwin, and the entire
Holt/Macmillan team. I am joyfully grateful to Mary Morgan for her beautiful illustrations.

Henry Holt and Company, LLC
*Publishers since 1866*
175 Fifth Avenue
New York, New York 10010
mackids.com

Library of Congress Cataloging-in-Publication Data
Engle, Margarita.
When you wander : a search-and-rescue dog story / Margarita Engle ; illustrated by Mary Morgan. — 1st ed.
p.   cm.
Summary: A dog that has just graduated from "sniffing school" advises readers what to do if they become lost in the woods,
and assures them that his smart nose will lead him to where they are. Includes facts about dogs' noses.
ISBN 978-0-8050-9312-4 (hardcover)
1. Search dogs—Juvenile fiction. [1. Search dogs—Fiction. 2. Dogs—Fiction. 3. Rescue work—Fiction. 4. Lost children—Fiction.]
I. Morgan, Mary, ill. II. Title.
PZ10.3.E58397Whe 2013  [E]—dc23  2012011491

First Edition—2013 / Designed by April Ward
The art for this book was created with watercolor, gouache, and colored pencils.
Printed in China by Macmillan Production Asia Ltd., Kowloon Bay, Hong Kong (Vendor Code: PS)

1  3  5  7  9  10  8  6  4  2

For Curtis and the dogs,
with love and hugs
—M. E.

To my beloved grandchildren,
Olivia Rose and Luca
—M. M.

I am a graduate
of sniffing school!

I practice sniffing
every day

just in case
you ever go out

in the woods

and lose
your way.

You smell
like wonderful
cinnamon cookie smiles
and your special
indoor forest
of toys
and hugs
and books.

When I sniff
your delicious shoes,
I can tell
that you love to run
on soft, green, roll-around
grass . . .

and I learn
that you love to jump
up and down
in squishy
snail-slime
mud.

When you wander
down a leafy path,
I can smell
your invisible
trail

of
happy
hops

and
skips

and—
oops.

My smart nose
tells me
where you
stopped
to sing
to a bird

and where
you danced
a little dance
with a bug.

My smart nose knows
when you are tired
and your sore feet
want to kick
your mean shoes.

If you get lost,
I will smell
your mixed-up
zigzag
back-and-forth
uphill
downhill
please-find-me
footsteps.

I can smell
the lonely night
and the whistling wind
and your wish
to be cozy
and safe
at home
in your own little forest
of toys
and hugs
and books.

If you are lost,
stay in one place.
Hug a tree.
Think of me.

I will race
against the night
and the wind
to bring you home
safe.

If you get lonely,
hug that tree!

Talk
to the tree.

Sing
to the tree!

**YELL**
at the tree.

Wait for me.

You will soon hear
the silvery singsong bell
that I wear on
my pretty collar.

You will see me
running toward you
wearing my bright orange
sniffing school vest.

You can hug me.

I will lick you.

I will help you.
I will bring people
to show you
the easy way
home.

Home,
where smiles
and hugs

and cookies . . .

and dreams
are waiting.

# DOG NOSE FACTS

- My nose is bigger than yours, and I have hundreds of scent receptor cells for each one of yours.

- My left and right nostrils can sniff separately, helping me follow the direction of a scent trail to its source.

- When I sniff a cookie, I can smell all the individual ingredients, including flour, sugar, butter, spices, baking powder, and salt.

- After a few minutes around smelly stuff, your nose stops paying attention, but my nose never gets tired.

- When I sniff a bush, a rock, or your shoe, I am smelling a story about all the animals and people who have passed by, or all the places where you have walked.

- When you feel nervous around dogs, I can smell your anxiety. So relax, and let me sniff your shoes!

# ADVICE FOR PARENTS AND TEACHERS

You can help search-and-rescue teams by teaching children to stay in one place if they get lost in the woods. The farther they wander, the harder they are to find. Please teach young people to choose a special tree friend to keep them company while they wait for a dog's smart nose to follow the invisible trail of human scent.